small stations fiction

Manuel Rivas
One Million Cows

Published in 2015 by
SMALL STATIONS PRESS
20 Dimitar Manov Street, 1408 Sofia, Bulgaria
You can order books and contact the publisher at
www.smallstations.com

This book was first published in the Galician language as *Un millón de vacas* by Edicións Xerais de Galicia (Vigo, 1989; enlarged edition, 2001). This translation follows the twelfth (2010) edition.

This work received a grant from the General Secretariat of Culture of the Ministry of Culture, Education and University Planning of the Xunta de Galicia in the call for translation grants of the year 2014.

Esta obra recibiu unha axuda da Secretaría Xeral de Cultura da Consellería de Cultura, Educación e Ordenación Universitaria da Xunta de Galicia na convocatoria de axudas para a tradución do ano 2014.

ISBN 978-954-384-035-9

Manuel Rivas

One Million Cows

Translated from Galician by **Jonathan Dunne**

Small Stations Press

Contents

For Toño, who introduced me to his sister

FIRST LOVE

Gaby, Gabriela, is older than me. I think she's a lot older.
Two years, at least. After such a long time, I wasn't
expecting to find her in the village, in Aita, but there she
was, sitting languidly on the Brandarices' stone bench, in
between two geranium pots.

'Hi.'

'Hi.'

'How are things?'

'Good. And you?'

'Good. Excellent. Actually, terrible.'

In reality, she was a lot older than me. Three years,
perhaps.

'You've got thinner.'

'You've got thinner as well.'

She was wearing a long skirt, and her feet were bare.
They were the large feet of a man.

'You've been away.'

'Yeah.'

'I might also be leaving.'

'Oh, really?'

'Yeah. I'm also leaving. I'm thinking of going on a trip. But far away, you know? To Australia or somewhere like that.'

'That would be great.'

'Yeah, I'm pretty sure I'll go to Australia. A friend of mine's parents are there. He's become a radio ham, and he talks to them at night.'

'I was in Barcelona, you know? Living with people and stuff.'

'Ah, Barcelona, right. I've never been on a trip, you know? I fancy doing something potent. Australia or something like that.'

'That would be amazing. So far away.'

'My friend reckons if you dug a hole from here to the other end of the earth, you'd come out in Australia. How was it in Barcelona?'

'Good. Well, OK. Pretty bad.'

'My friend gave me this watch. It wakes you up to the tune of "Happy Birthday". "Happy birthday to you"… It tells you the time in Tokyo, in London and in New York. And you can write down phone numbers and store them. It's like a computer. Here, have a look.'

'Oh, wow, that's fantastic. You know? I have a daughter.'

'A daughter?'

'Yeah. Do you want to see her?'

And she invited me in, smiling, as if it hurt her to smile.

MY COUSIN, THE GIGANTIC ROBOT

I got on his back and went cherry-picking.

I sometimes wondered whether Dombodán wasn't a robot Aunt Gala had bought in some junk shop at a knock-down price. One of those old robots Time gradually makes human, as it does trees, animals in the house, the radio with the wooden box that spoke hoarsely in the attic or the pantry where the apples were kept. But Dombodán, according to a secret shared by the family and everybody else, was a child my aunt had had out of wedlock.

Even so, when I was seated on his shoulders, up high, virtually kissing the red fruits of summer, I would pull on his ears in the secret hope he would reveal a bunch of multi-coloured wires like those in electronic toys that have been disembowelled. At this point, Dombodán's ears would begin to burn, and that for me was the sign his hidden circuits were on the verge of exploding. And explode, they did. He would drop me on the ground like a bothersome sack, howl like a rabid dog and grab hold of his ears.

That was all. He never responded with violence. He just started to ignore me, and I would land on the ground from the height of his back, which was like falling out of the sky. My gigantic cousin's passivity served only to confirm my suspicions that Dombodán was really a robot. The next opportunity I had, having gorged myself on cherries, I would go back to pulling on his ears with renewed vigour, convinced I would finally discover the hidden mechanisms responsible for activating his artificial intelligence. Never with any result.

There were electric batteries in the house, which were kept in a drawer of the dresser, in between some aspirins and some obituaries that had been cut out of the newspaper. A normal enough state of affairs, but one that didn't satisfy my logic. I examined all the household appliances in my grandpa's house and none of them, as far as I could tell, required batteries of such high voltage. When it was time for lunch, in between mouthfuls, I would observe Dombodán surreptitiously. Aunt Gala was far too careful, in my opinion, about his diet. He wasn't allowed to eat fried eggs and chips, something I found incomprehensible, since it was my favourite dish, he was forbidden pork, an obligatory source of nourishment for all the adults, and he was kept away from sweets as if they were the devil's own speciality. My surprise increased, since there was no way chicken broth could keep a giant's body going. During dessert, my aunt would bring a bottle the colour of smoked glass and give Dombodán a spoonful of a repugnant-looking oily liquid, which the giant willingly imbibed. This was obviously something to keep his circuits well greased, I thought. And it worked. Dombodán was the first to get up from the table, he undertook the heaviest tasks and wasn't in the accursed habit of having to sleep a siesta.

All my senses, during those childhood summers, were on high alert about Dombodán's behaviour. He never spoke, but I knew he wasn't completely mute because, according to my mother, on rare occasions he'd said unintelligible things more appropriate to Martians. What things? Strange things, my mother replied. My attempts to gain further information met with zero success. I asked other members of the family and realized they were avoiding the subject. Only one uncle of mine, from Seville, married to a sister of my mother and Aunt Gala's, revealed that Dombodán had once said the expression 'wee-wee' correctly. Having shared this with me, he burst out laughing, but for me this was a fact of the utmost importance. What other colloquialism could a robot be expected to come out with?

I never lost sight of Dombodán. I slowly realized his main point of contact in this world was my grandpa, who kept his other grandchildren, myself included, at a safe distance – not to mention the rest of my family, whom he appeared to openly despise. Grandpa Manuel was utterly deaf and had a carved walking stick he was always turning around, reason enough for him to inhabit his own, inaccessible universe. Only Dombodán was allowed to pass the barrier of his foul temper uninvited.

My grandpa couldn't hear, or so he gave us to understand, but with Dombodán he talked nineteen to the dozen. We only heard him, asking questions and giving the answers, while Dombodán watched carefully and nodded from time to time, as if partaking of some strange wisdom. One day, he talked to him about the war – a subject that put the adults on edge and was forbidden in conversations – and told him he'd known long before that all this was going to happen because early one winter's morning he'd seen two unknown birds, with gaudy colours and bloodshot eyes, sparring on a cart-track. Dombodán nodded and, from my hiding place, I wondered how a boy, however gigantic he may have been, could share such an old fool's vision.

An important moment in my inquiry was when it came time for bed. We little ones would be dressed in our pyjamas, made to pray to our guardian angel, and then told to go to sleep if we didn't want to get a hiding our own guardian angel couldn't save us from. From under the sheets, I kept a lookout. On one such night, I slipped out with all the stealth of an American Indian and waited for the decisive point at which Dombodán would be naked, convinced I would discover an articulated doll having his batteries removed so he could go to sleep. But then something very strange happened. The giant only took off his boots and fell on top of the bed with all his clothes on. The mystery was compounded by the fact there was no potty under his bed, which could only be because Dombodán didn't need to pee. Then Aunt Gala arrived and slowly undressed him, like somebody handling a toy. She took off her own clothes and began to caress him, caress him gently from top to toe, in a way that made me feel jealous.

There was a day in September when it always rained. The fire would be lit for the first time, and grandpa, without saying a word, twirling his stick like Charlie Chaplin, would sit in the corner nearest the hearth, ready to winter until the spring. All of us visitors would pack our bags, take the fruit offered by Aunt Gala and leave for the city. Dombodán looked sad, as if his circuits had gone rusty, and pressed his nose against the window facing the road.

THE SOLITARY SAILOR

Through the Singapore's window, the man with red hair had followed the storm's death throes. In its reckless convulsion, the sea vomited on the sand a frontier of remains, the sticky enchantment of seaweed, stateless sea urchins, evicted crustaceans and other things, a fairground of strange bodies, vessels with saltpetre and resin calligrams, errant mandibles, logs with wild animals, frayed ropes, machines with rusted teeth, single shoes and the skeleton of a watch. The sailor gestured in relief. The old sloop, the one with the black mast, had withstood the angry waves' assault in the shelter of the small fishing harbour.

The sun returned in triumph, and the ocean shone as far as the line of the horizon like the back of some colossal fish. People began to emerge. An old man half opened the door, seemed to hesitate, finally came in and put a coin in the slot-machine. He cursed under his breath. Gave the machine a slap on the side and left.

The Singapore bar was run by a fat man in his forties who occasionally disappeared into the kitchen, where he could be heard shouting. There were women's voices as well. A child clambered up the inside of the counter, balancing on the crates. He managed to get as high as the stranger and told him his father knew how to make miniature carts pulled by flies and also by butterflies, though these were more difficult, he said. The boy showed his arms covered in scratches and small bruises. He'd gone looking for nests and found two, he didn't know what birds they belonged to, but the eggs had blue spots and he'd smashed them right there, next to the quay. His father ordered him down from the counter and, before he could obey, slapped him on the head. The boy pursed his lips, climbed down and spat into the sawdust.

'I'm strong,' he said, looking at the sailor and again showing him the scratches from the brambles.

The fat man gave him another smack on the head, this time harder. The child kept his eyes fixed on the stranger. He started going red. He was going to cry, but tried not to. His tears betrayed him by spilling over. The air also betrayed him by pounding inside his chest. He started sobbing. His father walked to the other end of the bar, grabbed a broom and turned the television on, using the handle. The boy went to a table at the back and buried his face in his arms. His mother came out of the kitchen and shouted at him:

'Devil, you're a devil, why are you crying?'

Images of oriental peasants appeared on the screen, fleeing from soldiers who occasionally turned to wave at the camera. Sometimes, the colour faded and the scenes were shown in black and white. The fat man fiddled with the TV controls, using the end of the handle, but the colour had gone for good. There were large rice plantations being patrolled by helicopters, which cast their shadows on the fields. The boy had stopped crying and was gazing furtively at the sailor, who had a tattoo.

His father gestured energetically at the boy to come over. He lifted him off the ground and held him up to the television. The child fiddled with the knobs until the image improved and the colour returned. The fat man smiled. He lowered the child to the ground, ruffled his hair and gave him a friendly pat. The mother was watching from the door of the kitchen:

'I've told you before not to hit him on the head. Smack him on the bottom if you have to.'

The man didn't even look at her. Some music was playing outside. The sailor glanced in the direction of the window. A group of young people was sitting on an upturned boat. They had a large cassette player on the bow. They were all men, except for a woman with dyed hair. The owner of the Singapore spat into the sawdust:

'Drug addicts. They come and go. Take drugs.'

He grabbed the broom again and turned up the volume. The newsreader was giving the football results. The customers playing cards paid attention for the first time. The bar owner became animated. He seemed content with the results and gestured in triumph at the stranger.

'I also play football,' he said, enunciating his words loudly and clearly. 'I wasn't bad, no. So they said. I think I was quite good. I was good. Yes, good.'

He said it a couple of times until the red-haired sailor nodded, as if enjoying his victorious recollection. The bar owner pointed at the trophies on the shelves, in between the bottles of spirits, their metal gone rusty. He unhooked a photograph, wiped the dust off with the back of his hand, gazed at it in satisfaction and then showed it to the stranger. It was the portrait of a young man aged about twenty, who was fit-looking and strong. He was balancing his right foot on the ball. He wore blue shorts, a blue-and-white shirt and blue socks with white bands. He had long hair tied back in a ponytail. He was smiling.

'Nice kit, right?'

He hung the photograph back up, trying to make sure it coincided with the rectangle of dust on the wall. The stranger remained impassive, and this seemed to bother him. He pointed again at the footballer's portrait:

'That was me. That me. I was champion. And boss. Boss as well. Two years as boss. I tired. But look, that was me. That me.'

He placed a toothpick in his mouth and waited in vain for some commentary, some question:

'Shit. That was me.'

The man went off, muttering under his breath, to attend to some customers. The new arrivals ordered a bottle of champagne, and the bar owner served himself as well. They looked different from the other customers. They wore leather jackets, and the one who seemed to be the leader had his shirt unbuttoned, revealing a large, gold crucifix on his hairy chest. They were talking about women:

'I tell you, that boat needed five or six engines. I could only manage two.'

They cackled with laughter:

'But, Paco, only two?'

'What the fuck do you want? I was way over the limit and hadn't slept the night before. But I tell you, she could take at least five engines. Yours are going to drop off, they're so rusty. Listen up. One weekend, we have to leave our wives to take the children off somewhere, and I'll show you what is meant by a proper fuck.'

The Singapore's door reopened. A man with a moustache and a strong constitution approached the counter and called out to the owner in a voice loud enough to make the group in leather jackets fall quiet:

'I'm here about the job.'

The owner gazed at him slowly. He came out from behind the counter and gestured to him to follow. He drew a curtain and invited him to take a seat in the back room. He returned to his place behind the counter, and the members of the group went to join the new arrival.

The screen was showing images of preparations for an open-air art exhibition in a paved square surrounded by monumental façades. Cranes were moving large metal and stone sculptures. Nobody was watching. Only one old man looked up from his fanned-out cards when the machines raised a piece of granite similar to a millstone, but with an ox head set in the middle. The old man attracted the attention of the other card players.

'A load of bollocks,' declared one of them, and they went back to their game.

Broom at the ready, the Singapore's owner was trying now to switch channel. He looked for the child, but the child had disappeared. Some customers summoned him over, and he propped the broom in a corner. On the screen, a bearded man with a weary, melancholic air was talking about the death of a culture. He referred to the example of shooting stars, which vanish one night in seconds, having shone for thousands of years in the heavenly vault. Suddenly, emptiness. The Singapore's owner had regained his command post. He stroked his belly with his left hand and aimed the broom, this time successfully. On the screen appeared scenes of a sea storm. It was all immensely familiar. They were talking about the coast, this coast. Various boats were adrift, although, according to the Civil Defence spokesperson, everything was now under control. There'd been victims, including a solitary sailor. The news was accompanied by images of the sailor's ship, which had been smashed against the rocks, its black mast shattered. The cameras showed his lifeless, shipwrecked body, which had been carried on the back of waves towards the beach. He was a young man with red hair and a turtle tattoo.

There he was, his arms resting on the Singapore's counter. He gestured for another beer, but, far from serving him, the owner continued to stare at him. He raised one hand to his ear, rolled the toothpick between his lips and spat into the sawdust:

'That man on the television was you.'

The stranger nodded.

'It would seem you are dead.'

The visitor gestured to him that he was right.

'Affirmative?'

He nodded again.

The child was standing in front of the window, drawing things in the condensation. His father shouted to him to come over and lifted him on to the counter, opposite the sailor.

'See that man there. He's dead.'

And he gave him another friendly pat on the head.

A MATCH WITH THE IRISHMAN

At the height of my bunk, there's a calendar with a cow, and this makes me feel good. I sometimes fall asleep with my face pressed against the hull, seeking out the caress of a cold, rough hand. The sea ruminates a couple of inches away, and I experience a childish fear, the lazy sharpening of knives in the mouth of an expectant shark. The cow's image returns me to a domestic, protective world, the world of breath, smoke and an awakening house. I have nothing in common with the sea, except for the fact I'm on board, a member of the crew on the fishing boat *Lady Mary*, which sails under a British flag, once called *Our Lady* and based in Marín.

There are five Irishmen with us, apart from the captain, who is English. They don't appear to know much about fishing, but they're here on account of the laws regulating the Gran Sol. One person who is knowledgeable is Vilariño, a skipper from Ribeira. One of the Irishmen, the youngest, has been with me for two days, stuck in the cabin, because he slashed his hand open with a knife for beheading fish. There's absolutely nothing wrong with me, just a demon in my insides, but Vilariño the skipper said, 'Go on, boy, go under deck, wrap yourself in a blanket and, whatever happens, don't move from your bed.'

Vilariño seems like a good guy, though he is a bit strange. He doesn't drink, he doesn't smoke, he doesn't swear and he doesn't address people by their nicknames. What's more, he prays. He can hardly be called a Christian. The first night, after we left port, he let me stay on the bridge, watching the radar. I've always been fascinated by machines with light. Vilariño kept quiet, seemingly alert, as if he were expecting to hear some familiar message behind the radio interference.

It wasn't that. 'Let's shut this henhouse down,' he said. And he turned it off. His cabin was a small room on the bridge itself, and in he went, so he said, to check the route on the map. But shortly afterwards I heard a murmur, something like a distant voice refusing to leave the radio. I stuck my ear to the door. Vilariño was praying, as if talking to somebody. I'd never heard a man pray like that. I mentioned it to Touro, the cook, and he confessed very secretively that Vilariño was a strange one:

'He's a Protestant. That's why he prays.'

The Irishman who's with me in the cabin, the youngest, as I said, has a gold earring and hair so long he ties it in a ponytail. I'm wrapped in my blanket, trying to curl up into a ball, so that my head touches my knees, but not him. He barely sleeps, stretches out on the bed and lets his head fall out, with his eyes wide open.

The Irishman listens to music, or so he says, but all I can hear is the gnashing of the large fish's teeth a couple of inches from my head. I try to make him understand, but he's unaware of the danger. He points towards the cow, the one in the *Provisions and Supplies* almanac, and almost makes me laugh. 'No, for fuck's sake, a fish with a mouth this big.' He looks incredulous and goes back to his music.

'They're all Gypsies,' said Touro distrustfully. 'Blond Gypsies, but Gypsies all the same.' They were from the same family and had come on board together. 'Not a fucking clue about fish,' the cook went on, 'but you watch out for them, they're like foxes. No playing games. If you're not careful, they'll have the shirt off your back.' I've been with him for too long, however, the one with the earring, who wakes me up with a couple of pats, just as the shark is about to pierce the hull, a couple of inches from my head and petrified eyes. The Irishman gestures to me with a dice box. To begin with, I'm not sure, but something pushes me forwards. After all, he looks friendly enough and, if I carry on like this, feeling bewitched, with that rabid animal on the verge of gnawing at my imagination, my head will explode.

'Don't say I didn't warn you,' Touro will probably remark. I don't have anything left. The Irishman moves his healthy hand with all the skill of a Tafur. 'It's all over, mate, I don't have a penny left.' That is when he points to the cow. 'The cow? You want to bet the cow? A note for the cow? OK.' He smiles in satisfaction. Two rolls: full house, aces over kings. My hand is trembling. Heavens above! Five of a kind!! With the cow on my lap, I get back everything I've lost and win whatever he's prepared to risk. We don't say a word. The Irishman goes back to his bunk, and I remain sitting, crying in silence, the cow staring at me.

The big fish doesn't appear all night. It has stopped gnawing at the hull, a couple of inches from my head. I now know what the sound of the sea is like, the coming and going of a weary mammal, and feel content. I go up on deck. The others are working in the mist, and I join them with renewed vigour. I am able to behead the fish without throwing up or looking horrified. Vilariño comes up and pats me on the neck:

'I thought you were going to lose your mind, boy, I thought you were going to lose your mind.'

THE LAME HORSE'S ROAD

I used to make that trip every Friday afternoon. It was a hellish route, but I wanted to arrive as soon as possible. The road from Muros, having clambered up the mountainside, burnt by sea and man, crosses a long, green desert. Or so it seems. I could only remember one involuntary stop. A herd of horses ignored my horn. They stood in the middle of the road, savouring the wind on their lips. From time to time, they would jerk their necks with picaresque elegance and beat their hooves like a kind of challenge. I made another useless attempt to clear the way with my horn. Patience. They also seemed to be waiting.

From among the pines, preceded by a loud whinny, appeared a handsome, black stallion. It took up position in the middle of the road and slowly made its way towards the vehicle. It eyed me with lofty indifference and then went around the car, as if making an inspection. Finally it returned to the group, nodded its head and ordered the herd to a field on the left-hand side, in the direction of the ocean's balconies. The boss walked majestically. It was lame. It wasn't me they were after.

What happened today is another story.

In front was a car with a foreign number plate and then, with their backs towards us, a crowd of people. They advanced slowly, with heavy feet, filling the breadth of the road underneath a leaden sky. With the car going at a man's pace, I realized how much the track revealed its entrails of gravel and mud. In the delayed panorama, the eyes followed the line of electric fences, drawn from time to time, in the ditch, to the rusty remains of domestic appliances or, on the horizon, to scraggy, discoloured scarecrows and cows that looked as if they'd been waiting for that moment for centuries. Leaning against a gate, a child followed the silent procession with his gaze. His head was shaved, revealing white spots, and he wore a blue jacket with elbow patches and a badge sewn with golden thread. I noticed it, its embroidery, and he stared at me with innocent pride.

The people in the car in front were becoming impatient. They were young, and one of them, the co-pilot, had been gesturing animatedly for some time. They blasted the horn. Intermittently to begin with, but then with greater intensity. The last row of the procession ended up turning around. They came to a halt. They were aged men and women, even those who didn't look so old, all carrying black umbrellas and farmers' sticks. They eyed us sombrely, me as well. And that sufficed.

Behind remained the stone houses of the discreet locality the procession must have started from. Further on, nothing, just the long, straight road and an increasingly turbulent sky. So when it rained, it did so methodically.

The people in the procession opened their umbrellas while some of them covered their heads with raincoats. Instead of quickening their pace, they slowed down. It was necessary to stop the car and proceed by fits and starts, in short bursts. The rain covered the windscreen, and I amused myself by avoiding the puddles, as in a winter's video game.

From the cluster of people, a shadow peeled off. The car in front carried on, but I decided to stop. Having settled down, the man removed his beret, which was glistening with water, and coughed. He coughed with a deep-seated cough that seemed to have no end. He wiped his mouth with a handkerchief, breathed in heavily, glanced at me sideways and lit a cigarette. He offered me one. 'Smoking's good for colds,' he remarked confidently. And then he spat out the first threads of tobacco, 'Damn priest.'

He fell silent for a moment, as if he regretted being indiscreet. He glanced at me again.

'In winter, we old people fall down like birds, but this one was young, young and in good health. Such is life, I suppose.'

'Why?' I asked.

'Excuse me?' he replied distrustfully.

'Why did you swear about the priest?'

The priest had refused to bury the dead man in the parish. The whole village was indignant, he'd been an extremely good person and hung himself from an apple tree. The priest said according to the laws of the Church he couldn't give him a Christian burial, so they were taking him to another parish three miles further on.

'What if they don't bury him there?'

The old man clicked his tongue. Kept glancing out of the corner of his eye.

'You know? The winters are getting colder.'

The procession stopped before the yard of a small, Romanesque church with poorly plastered walls. A fracture in the rose window on the façade had been repaired using bricks, and next to the bell stood a loudspeaker.

'Here we are,' said the old man.

He got out of the car and gestured a hasty farewell, enveloped in a cloud of smoke and mist. Something made me park. A group of neighbours, standing near the coffin, seemed to take the initiative, talking amongst themselves. There were a few, long minutes of waiting, the water pouring down the parishioners' faces, and, just as I was about to set off again, the old man pointed towards me.

'Friend, we need a car,' said one of the leaders of the procession. 'We have to go and fetch the priest before he does a runner.'

We drove down slippery cart-tracks until reaching a manor house half in ruins. An enormous mastiff came out to meet us with hostile words. The old man gave it a cursory whack, and the dog fled with a whimper. The door of the house opened, and I had to stop myself fleeing with my look. There was a repulsive creature, a hunchbacked woman with only one good eye. The old man asked for the priest, and she replied with a kind of grunt. I felt my insides churn. Finally a young man with an angelic face appeared, almost a child in a cassock.

'I know why you're here, but he didn't die in a state of grace.'

'He was a good person, reverend father,' replied the old man.

I realized my first impression had been deceptive. This priest with the appearance of a child had a cold disposition, steely grey eyes. He seemed to ponder. He glanced at the monstrous woman, who gestured her assent.

'Very well then. May the Lord Jesus Christ be my guide.'

On the way, no one spoke. When we arrived, the coffin had been placed on a flagstone in the churchyard and the neighbours were waiting in the shelter of the cemetery walls. Inside the church it was cold, colder than outside. The priest's prayers were followed by a chorus of splutters. Suddenly there was the most absolute silence. The pater stared down at his parishioners.

'He didn't die at peace with God. What's more, it will be difficult for him to enter the kingdom of heaven, since whoever denies life denies God. Life is a gift from Our Lord, and only he can decide the moment of our death. There isn't much hope for you either. You live in sin, you're lost creatures poisoned by temptations of the flesh. Don't think he deserves mercy or forgiveness. What he did was an act of arrogance and selfishness in the face of Our Lord. I shall pray for you too, but I don't suppose it will do much good.'

Having said this, he glared at us, turned around and continued with the service. When we came out of the church, having deposited the dead man underground, the neighbours wandered down the road in scattered groups. The old man took his leave again in his own way.

'He said terrible things to you,' I remarked, almost shouting.

'The whole time in church I was trying to wiggle my toes,' said the old man. 'I was worried because I couldn't feel them.'

'What the priest said! You shouldn't allow it,' I insisted in a rage.

'Carry on your way, friend.'

The night seemed to cascade out of the womb of that leaden sky. The old man limped off in a cloud of smoke and rain.

ONE OF THOSE GUYS WHO COME FROM FAR AWAY

'Look, look. He's an amazing guy. He doesn't talk. He's unbelievable. He doesn't say a word. His name is Dombodán.'

Marga had got herself a fine acquisition and was determined, as always, to introduce him with a flourish. Everybody turned to look at the seven-foot giant, who smiled shyly. 'Wherever did you find such a perfect specimen?' asked Rita, the little bitch. Everybody laughed at the joke. 'He fell straight out of the sky into my bed, darling,' said Marga, affectionately interlocking arms with the giant. 'And I'm not going to share him.' Having said this, she led him towards the bar.

'Did you see that guy?' asked Rita. 'He smells bad.' 'In this day and age, still wearing a corduroy jacket,' remarked Pachi. 'He's covered in dandruff,' observed Virxinia. Raúl had a doubt: 'Does he not talk, or is he dumb?' 'That girl,' complained Marijé, 'no longer knows what to do to surprise us. First, she hooks up with an Arab and now she brings along a country bumpkin. Do you think she's taken him to bed yet?'

'Anyway, he smells bad,' added Rita.

Marga returned with the look of somebody in love. Her companion was savouring a beer. A layer of foam stuck to his reddish chin. He smiled in the direction of the group. He looked like a real idiot. 'Listen,' said Raúl, 'is that guy normal?' 'He doesn't talk, that's all there is to it. He occasionally says things. Every now and then. He's amazing,' declared Marga, embracing the world with her arms. Raúl stared at the others and gestured in resignation. 'Looks like we'll have to put up with him.'

Just to be annoying, Rita hopped into Marga's white sports car. She sat in the back and leaned over towards Dombodán with a friendly air. 'Don't be offended, big guy, they're just jokes. We're really very nice. Isn't that so, Marga?' Raúl overtook them and honked his horn twice. His car raised a curtain of water. It was raining cats and dogs that night. After they'd left the city, everything before them was a cave. 'You'll see,' said Marga, addressing Dombodán sweetly, 'Raúl will get there first and light a fire. It'll be a wonderful night.' Rita was strangely silent. 'They should wear white,' said Marga. 'What?' Rita was slow to ask. 'Those peasants should wear white. They always dress in mourning, with their black umbrellas, like crows. You never see them until you're almost on top of them. And sometimes they even have cows. Where on earth can they be going with a cow at this hour of the night?' 'Yes,' murmured Rita, 'you're right.'

When they reached the house in the country, the lights inside were on and music was playing. The sea was very close. 'I sometimes think it's like an animal,' said Marga, running towards the porch. 'Like what?' 'The sea, like an animal.' In the lounge, Raúl was uncorking a bottle to the sound of merriment. 'In you go, go on,' Marga gave Dombodán a gentle shove. 'This is Raúl's parents' holiday home.' She stood on tiptoe to whisper in his ear, 'They're loaded. His father was in the army, but they're rolling in it.' In a corner, Marijé was seated between some cushions, humming along to the music and moving her head. Rita went over. 'What a strange guy!' 'Who?' 'Marga's big boy.' 'Oh, him. Yeah, he doesn't speak.' 'No, not because of that. He has scales.' 'You what?' 'It's not dandruff on his jacket. They're fish scales.'

'You like it, right?' Dombodán was staring at the fire and jumped when Raúl slapped him hard on the back. Then he smiled and nodded. 'I once had a mute friend,' the host went on, 'and he was extremely sensitive.' He was now addressing everyone, 'Virgo was a special guy. He couldn't speak, but he could mimic animals. He did it brilliantly. One night we were out binging, right in the city centre, he started crowing like a cockerel, exactly like a cockerel. Again and again, getting louder all the time. Lights started to go on, and people came out on to their balconies. Since Virgo had no other way of replying, he started pissing in the street. Right there. One old woman shouted that the end of the world had come. And then it got light.'

The sea also penetrated the cracks now, with its smell of fresh urine. The group mixed champagne with the smoke of hashish. Dombodán declined. 'Fuck, that's just we need, the guy's a bore and a prig,' remarked Pachi.

'He has something better,' said Marga with a knowing wink. She stuck her hand in Dombodán's jacket and rummaged around in the inside pocket. She pulled out a small bag, which she carefully opened. 'Fuck, fuck, it's coke.' The whole group surrounded her. 'I swear it's the best I've ever tried,' declared Marga. Dombodán carried on staring at the fire, as if oblivious to everything. 'You scored there, big boy. Don't tell me you smuggle the stuff?' Dombodán didn't join the party this time either. 'He wants to sleep. When he gets like that, it's because he wants to sleep,' said Marga, stroking him.

He woke up because something sticky had slithered across his hands. Dombodán shouted. It was a strange shout, too high-pitched for such a rotund body. He shook his arms and ran with panicky clumsiness towards a corner. The reptile followed him, as if drawn by his terror. Dombodán shrieked again. It was a piercing, prolonged cry. His eyes were swallowed up in anguish. It was then the others emerged from their hiding place, roaring with laughter. Raúl picked up the snake and kissed it on the mouth. Dombodán was trembling on his knees. 'Poor thing,' said Marga.

They were now involved in a new game. Raúl took down the cages of white mice. Everybody stood expectantly at the starting line, having closed all the doors in the lounge. Raúl opened the cages and drove the animals out. 'After them!' They all laughed, sweating, their eyes ablaze. The rodents, being pursued by brooms and high heels, sought out the furthest corners. One crouched at Dombodán's feet, stiff and staring into the distance. Raúl crept up behind it. Everybody abandoned the chase in order to watch the hunt. His hands were big and hairy on the back. At the last moment, he threw himself on top of the animal. 'Fuck, the animal bit me!' The others laughed. 'Fucking hell, it stuck its teeth in, the little shit.' Dombodán stared off into the distance. The mouse remained at his feet. 'Just you wait and see, you bastard.'

Raúl opened one of the doors and bounded up the stairs. He came back with a revolver. 'For fuck's sake, Raúl, calm down.' 'No fucking way, this rodent's had its chance.' He aimed slowly, gripping the butt in both hands. He fired once. Twice. And a third time. The animal didn't even move, clinging to Dombodán's boots. The blood looked redder against the white skin. All that could be heard was the sea. In the long silence, the other mice came out of their nooks and crannies and returned to the cages, with their heads bowed.

'Right, that's enough, let's have a drink. For fuck's sake, this is supposed to be a party,' bellowed Raúl in a voice that sounded like a command. 'You too, calamity, drink something.' Dombodán obeyed. He emptied a glass in one go and filled it up again. 'Hey, looks like he's waking up.' The jokes returned, together with the music. Raúl went up to Marga and embraced her from behind. He kissed her on the back of her neck. Shortly after that, they left the room.

Dombodán had gone back to the fire, the glass in his hand. Rita sat down next to him. 'He's fucking her, you know.' Dombodán shrugged his shoulders. 'Don't you care that they're doing it right in front of your nose?'

He remained unmoved. In front of his nose was only the crackle of the logs. 'I'm tired of all this stuff, you know, but it's the way things are. If you don't defend yourself, if you're not hard, everybody walks all over you. I couldn't give a damn about Raúl. Deep down, he's just a spoiled brat, but he's so sure about what he does that everything goes well for him. Did you know he has a girlfriend? Well, he does, but he never brings her to these parties. He laughs at her, says she's stupid, she doesn't want to sleep with him until they get married. He takes her home early and then joins the gang. But he's been with her for two years, and I'm sure he won't leave her. He controls himself. I'm different. At university, we're out having fun every night. Raúl was always one of the crowd, but, when it's time for the exams, he controls himself. He shuts himself away, refuses to see anybody and then passes. I'm different. I carry on partying until the night before. If you're a certain way, you have to be like that always and not control yourself like a hypocrite. For example, I had an abortion. That's right, I had an abortion. The guy who was with me encouraged me. "It's the best for both of us, especially for you, girl," he said. Do you know what he did? When it came down to it, he ran away, the little coward. "It's your business, girl, you brought it upon yourself. Do the best you can." As if he'd never known me, the little bastard. Listen, it must be very sad not being able to speak.'

Raúl came back, stretching his arms. He slapped Dombodán on the neck a couple of times. Dombodán carried on sitting there, drinking in front of the fire. 'Feeling better, big boy?' Marga opened the blinds. It was getting light. 'Oh, look how beautiful.' It was beautiful. The tireless, old animal roaring on the sand. 'To the beach, everybody to the beach!' shouted Raúl.

There they were, wrapped in blankets, sitting in a circle. They had bags under their eyes, and the wind tossed their hair over their faces. 'We look like a tribe,' remarked Pachi. 'I have one last game for you,' said Raúl. 'No more games, Raúl, please,' said Marga. 'Just one. A real game.'

Raúl pulled out the revolver. 'Listen, there's only one bullet inside. You've all heard of Russian roulette, haven't you? My father did it loads of times in Africa. A lieutenant in the legion died like this, with two pairs of balls. There's only one bullet, we pass it to each other, and whoever gets the bullet, goodbye. I've already drawn lots. Dombodán, you're the last.' Everybody recognized the wink of complicity. 'Don't worry, nothing's going to happen,' Raúl hinted with his eyes, 'we're just going to make fun of this enormous idiot.'

The revolver went from one person to another. They aimed at their temples, and the trigger made a dull sound. They then breathed out dramatically. It was Dombodán's turn. He stared at them all, one after the other. Pursed his lips. Lifted the revolver and pulled the trigger. Another dull sound. Dombodán stared at them now as he'd never stared before, with hatred. He opened the chamber. There wasn't a bullet inside. 'Shit,' he spat in the sand. 'You hear?

'Shit,' said the mute. 'You're all a pile of shit.'

He marched in the direction of the sea. Against the horizon, his back looked broader than ever. Hanging in the sky, comic and tragic, the seagulls.

THE ENGLISHMAN

In that corner of fishermen, his world was a shotgun. He lived alone with his mother in a house without a granary or nets, beside the mud-flats and lagoon of Mindoao. He used to hunt for rabbits and foxes on the white hills and especially, when it was season, for mallards, coots, moorhens, teals and even the odd heron (which he would desiccate and sell) on that sweet sea where the wind was lulled to sleep by the rushes. There, among the reeds, he'd grown up, and no one in Porto Bremón dared challenge him for that kingdom.

As a young man, he was a drunkard, full of bravado and craziness. His nickname at the time was Red. On the night before his departure, he swore to his friends he would return from England a rich man.

'I'll come back a gentleman, and you'll still be a bunch of ruffians,' he declared, and no one dared refute him, even if just because it's not nice to contradict a drunk who may never show his face again.

But Red did return after several years. He'd changed a lot in the way he behaved, as if he'd calmed down. He appeared to be accustomed to money, but wasn't showy and, with a measure of humility, he even affirmed that people there earned more than here, but not so much as was said. He did, however, declare he'd learned how to play golf and acquired a taste for horse racing.

He would go to the Porto café for breakfast and order fried eggs with ham together with his coffee, to the consternation of the fishermen who used to start the new day with a tipple of brandy or rum. He dressed elegantly, but not in the old style. He wore a tie on top of a coloured shirt and shoes with a distinctive toecap, different from the rest. But he certainly wasn't the kind of person to keep his distance. His old friends would say that golf was for pussies, at which point he would stand up straight, ask Leonor, the owner of the Porto, for a brush, grab it by the handle and, after calculated movements, chip a cork through the half-open door. Not long afterwards, most of the clientele had had a go with all sorts of objects, raising clouds of sawdust and knocking bottle tops against the windows. Red, who was now nicknamed the Englishman, laughed and affirmed that the day would come when Porto Bremón had its own golf course with long, green fairways, smooth as the head of a conscript, and perfect holes indicated by flagsticks.

'The ducks stopping over on Mindoao lagoon will settle there, and you'll be able to hunt them from the terrace while sipping your vermouth.'

But that was not the full extent of his projects. Over consecutive summer visits, he educated the locals about the advantages of science, including new gardening techniques. Every house in England, he said, had grass and flowering plants in the front, not like here, where the running water was dirty and everything was filthy in winter and full of flies in summer. And he embellished stories of men who spent their Sunday mornings pruning and industrious women who hung lace curtains on the windows while a Sunday cake turned golden in the oven.

'It won't be like that where there are sailors,' insisted one of those present.

'It's like that everywhere,' declared the Englishman.

This initial objection encouraged the others.

'So why are they still in Gibraltar?' asked the most political.

'I heard on TV that, in English schools, they beat the children until they bleed,' informed another.

'And don't they drive on the wrong side?' asked a third ironically.

The Englishman moistened his lips, gauged the distance and gave a precise hit with the brush.

When he made up his mind to return for good, the Englishman became a kind of honorary consul who attended to the few visitors that came to those parts. He stopped improvising speeches about civic training, and all his efforts seemed now to be practically oriented. He wanted to be rich, the richest man in Porto Bremón, and he achieved this. Up until then, the fishermen had sold their fish and shellfish to an intermediary who arrived from the capital and decided on the price. The difficulties of transport and the lack of competition made him essential. The Englishman got hold of a refrigerated lorry, offered more advantageous prices and, by becoming the only purchaser, fixed his own terms. At the same time, he discovered something everybody already knew: what people in Porto Bremón really liked wasn't fish, but pork chops. And so he opened the first butcher's.

There were lots of things waiting to be discovered in those new times. For example, the thing that attracts the most at night is illumination. In the darkness of a seaside town, neon lights are irresistible. The Porto's sign became like a sad altar-lamp when the Englishman opened the Trafalgar, which shone with flashing lights, game machines and a jukebox. Even the oldest residents couldn't resist the fascination of this establishment full of luminous charms, gleaming wall fixtures and stunning marquetry, and came to lean on the metal counter like moths.

The Trafalgar was followed by a disco of the same name, frequented by young people from all around, who didn't have to travel to more distant towns. The building, owing to its novelties, such as those taps with photoelectric cells that turn on automatically when you put your hands under them, was a talking point for months. Porto Bremón became known as a summer resort, something he encouraged, and took advantage of, by opening a restaurant with rooms and later erecting a block of apartments. Everybody called him 'Mister', and what had started as a joke became thoroughly accepted, to the extent that few remembered now where he'd come from. His parents had died, he had no known relatives, and some of his habits, such as bathing in the sea in winter or taking a short-tailed dog for a walk every evening, cloaked him in a strange myth, according to which he was a castaway spat up in a storm, who had chosen to settle on that wild coast for good.

The Englishman's finest hour came when a golf course was inaugurated as part of Porto Bremón's tourist complex. It was a glorious Sunday morning. The powers that be surrounded him and vied for his attention. Authorities had travelled from the capital. Everybody smiled when the band struck up a march of the British royal family in his honour. As they went around, the governor waxed lyrical about the lawn stretching out like a velvet blanket, in sharp contrast to the imposing lunar landscape of sand and stone on either side.

'It won't be easy to keep it as green as this,' remarked the governor.

'No problem, it will always be green,' he replied.

He knew this better than anyone. They were walking on top of a sweet sea dreamed by itinerant birds in cold lands. Buried beneath their feet, the mud-flats and lagoon of Mindoao.

LEAVE NOTHING BEHIND

He had sworn never to buy his son a toy weapon.

He had belonged to Greenpeace, he still paid an annual subscription, and felt a pang of nostalgia when he saw a pacifist march on television defy a ban on entering the Nevada desert, where nuclear engineers were going crazy sowing monstrous fungi in craters. His work as a sales rep kept him very busy. He'd also got married. And had a child.

'A child?' asked Nicolás, his eyes open in horror. Nicolás was someone he'd shared old concerns with and bumped into at the airport.

'Well, yes,' he said, feeling somewhat uncomfortable. He'd never considered these things needed explaining. You just have a child, and that's it.

'Don't get me wrong, I mean it involves a lot of courage. I think you have to be very brave to have a child. I could never reach a decision like that. It would make me feel giddy.'

He'd never really thought that much about the meaning of having a child. He'd got married because he felt like it, and had a child for the same reason. Nicolás, however, continued to stare at him like a confessor tormented by the sins of others.

'Well, I think most of all you have to consider it a biological fact, without giving it too much transcendence. It's a way of assuming our animal condition. A child makes you feel good, that's all, like an animal. You recover your animal nature as something positive.'

Nicolás laughed. After all, he was a biologist.

'Maybe. For me, it's a bit like making yourself out to be God for a moment. Bringing someone into this world must be beautiful, but... it's also terrible. Don't you think?'

'Listen. He wakes up all the time at night. Calls out to us, and goes back to sleep. A couple of times a night. You may well be a god, but you're pretty messed up. Not like him. He just sleeps whenever he wants to.'

Now the two of them laughed.

'Do you tell him stories?'

'Oh, yes, I've told him thousands. At least, whenever I'm there. You know I'm always on the move with this stupid job. There are nights I tell him three or four, and fall asleep before he does.'

'What kind of stories?' asked Nicolás with amusement.

'Oh, I don't know, mostly about animals. He loves stories that have to do with animals. Animals with young, and along come the hunters, that kind of stuff. I try to make sure the wolf is a good one,' he added with a sly wink.

'I'd like to meet him some time,' declared Nicolás as they were leaving.

His friend waved goodbye one last time from behind the glass door, and the other headed for one of the airport shops. He always took his son back a present. There wasn't much to choose from. The largest selection was of imitation firearms. There were all kinds: the cowboy's Colt, a special agent's pistol with a silencer, a rifle with a telescopic sight, a machine gun with laser beams. And then the artillery, armoured vehicles and highly sophisticated advances in star wars technology. He dismissed them all with a look of disgust and finally opted for a small umbrella made of transparent plastic, with stickers of funny, little animals.

When he got home, the child was already asleep.

'I brought him this,' he said with a smile.

'It's nice,' remarked his wife.

In the morning, the child asked, 'Are you going to work?' He said that he was, sadly, and the child burst into tears.

'I brought you something,' said his father, jumping out of bed. The child fell silent and waited expectantly for him to unwrap the present.

'Look, it has pictures of Snoopy,' said his father with satisfaction, holding out the umbrella.

The child looked at the umbrella, turned it over so he could see all the animals, and appeared content.

Before leaving, he gave him a kiss and a pat on the head. As he was opening the door, he heard his son calling out to him. He turned around and saw him standing there, with one foot forward and the umbrella pressed against his shoulder with all the expertise of a marksman.

'Bang, bang! Daddy, you're dead.'

GOATS DON'T CRY

The white swan came over, asking for food in its piggish voice. He missed it, and the remains of his cigarette were extinguished by the obscenely clean waters of Lake Geneva, which he always praised in front of his family and friends when he returned to the village for the local festivities or at Christmas. The head of personnel at the Hotel Chateau Blanc wasn't pleased to hear that he was leaving for good. He'd been an exemplary employee. The head of personnel knew this, and so did he. His first job, when he was almost a child, had been to wash the dishes of those who wash the dishes. Now, on reception, he was able to hold a conversation with an opera singer and for her to be so entranced she left a generous tip and a flower in his name.

It was two weeks since he'd received a letter from his sister Mercedes. To tell the truth, she was the only one who ever wrote. The others were far too lazy, not a single postcard in fifteen years. At the festivities, they were pleasant enough, drunk as lords, asking him again and again, 'So, Luisiño, how much do you earn now that you've stopped washing the dishes... So, Luisiño, how much do you earn now that you're in charge of the lift... So, Luisiño, you must be rich now that you're on first-name terms with everybody...' Mercedes did what she could, 'I'm writing to let you know everything is fine, you'll have heard Lorenzo's daughter, the one who works at the hospital, got married, I suppose everything is well where you are, though we saw on television it was very cold.' The wretched beasts couldn't even imagine the joy he felt when he saw Mercedes' spindly handwriting, those letters threaded together like the stitches of a rag.

And yet this letter from two weeks ago had broken his heart. The hotel was warm as toast, and it was snowing outside. He opened a window and held out his hands. He was unable to cry. He felt the snow melting between his fingers until it formed a pool, which he lifted to his face. His grandmother had told him there were two kinds of eyes incapable of crying. Those of the devil and those of a goat. He knew perfectly well what it said in the letter, but he reread it anyway. 'You'll know we agreed to sell the lands and house in Penaverde, since a very good buyer turned up from La Coruña, whom mother liked a lot. She'll go to live in Orense with Benito. All we need now is your signature, so it would be good if you could come during Holy Week and we can all go to the solicitor together.' Mercedes, Mercediñas, didn't even send him her love. She must have thought it unnecessary, since they'd all been together not so long ago, on Christmas Eve in Penaverde. Ah, Mercedes, Mercediñas, you're just like the rest, you kept silent like a whore, because that buyer from Coruña must have been hanging around for a while, he can't have turned up out of the blue. And mother, bedraggled fly, more dead than alive, what on earth could she say?

He took his leave of the staff – Rosa from Portugal, who wept as if a son of hers was going off to war, and Mr Fulvio, the head of personnel, who being Italian wasn't stupid and gave him the kind of hug no square-headed Swissman would ever give. 'You know where we are,' the Italian had said. He'd have cried were it not for the fact that goats don't cry. He put on some sunglasses for driving along the white roads and started on his way.

He didn't plan to stop. He knew he wasn't going to stop, just to drink some coffee and take a leak. He surprised himself, however, without doing either, at the gates of Penaverde. He realized he'd been turning corners for some time in a sleepy state of mind when he noticed on the radio they were saying it was summer in Mar del Plata. 'Lucky you,' joked the presenter. 'Aren't we just?' replied the man at the other end of the line. Then came the signature tune. The programme was called *Galicia in the World*. He parked in Vilar Cross. He felt dizzy, as if he'd been smoking non-stop for two days. The sky here was much lower than in Switzerland. If you didn't get down on your knees, you ran the risk of having the clouds make off with your head. He closed his eyes. Everything, including the trees, had a tired gleam, like an altar covered in candles that have been burning for years.

He felt unable to get back in the car. He started walking along the old track, stumbling so much he thought he'd have to learn how to walk again. He immersed himself in the stream coming from Castro, which formed a pool in Baixa, where the alder spread its shade, and felt relief from the lively bubbling on the soles of his feet. The brambles had spread over that path long since abandoned by defunct carts, catching at his clothes like flailing arms. This gave him strength. He started treading firmly, walking on the clods of earth with his head held high, until he reached the front of the house in Penaverde. He stopped, slowly shaking his head with painful eyes. This is what the sun does when it goes down. Everything was dead. There was no dog barking or smoke forming branches. That was when he took a leak and missed not having a coffee, still unable to cry.

A TRIP TO THE MARKET

'I pay you to tell me when I'm making a fool of myself and not to spend the whole day patting me on the back,' said the candidate.

'I didn't know you were afraid of fish eyes,' replied the adviser.

'I'm not afraid of them. I just can't bear them, that's all.'

'You turned away. Nothing else. I don't think that will lose you any votes.'

'But the woman realized. When I offered her my hand, she looked at me distrustfully, like someone who's discovered an undesirable secret.'

'You're just worried because it's the end of the campaign. You're tired. Nothing else.'

'I don't know how I could have given her my hand. She wiped hers on her apron. But it still had scales.'

'She was a fishmonger, a bearded fishwife. Nothing else.'

'There was a prolonged silence. Like in a photograph.'

'The people were with you. I don't think anyone likes watching how they gouge out the eyes of fish.'

'They looked alive. The eyes, I mean. So open and with that look of bewilderment… It must be a horrible way to die, if you're a fish. I sometimes wonder which is worse: to die from a lack of air or from too much of it.'

'…'

'Why are you laughing?'

'You are the answer to that dilemma. Neither too little, nor too much. Just the right amount. Everybody goes along with that electoral proposal. Just the right amount of air to live.'

'I managed to smile when I finally shook hands with the fishwife. Even though she was bearded and had scales on her hands.'

'Never give up on that smile. Especially when you have nothing to say.'

'I found it so difficult, particularly when that guy, the pig farmer, laid into me. I was trying to remember what we'd said in the manifesto about the price of pig meat. But it was impossible to reason.'

'Better that way. In the manifesto, we said it would no longer be profitable to raise pigs.'

'I think he would have killed me right there and then. He shouted out terrible things, always in relation to pigs. But I still managed to smile.'

'That's what you do best. Nobody smiles like you.'

'But sometimes I feel insecure. I don't know. Do you think it's right to smile when you're being attacked by a crazy pig farmer who's gone out of his mind?'

'It would be worse to tell him what was written in the manifesto. The technical department reached the conclusion we can't keep on subsidizing pig farming. According to them, it would be more profitable to buy all the farms and close them down.'

'I think he wanted to kill me. He twisted his beret like the neck of a bird. But I still smiled. Like that Gypsy who wanted to tell my fortune. I gave her a thousand pesetas, but didn't show her my hand. Her eyes were the colour of ash.'

'That detail looked really good in front of the cameras.'

'Do you think we'll win?' asked the candidate.

'Of course we will,' said the adviser.

ONE MILLION COWS

She was dressed not in black, but in a blue and white print dress, with a shawl the colour of old silver, like a continuation of her hair. She gestured to me to stop from inside the bus shelter and, when I did so, peered in through the window of the car with eyes like those of a barn owl, behind tortoiseshell glasses.

'So are you going to Vigo, or not?'

She asked this as if there really were no other place to go. 'Thank you, son, you're a life saver,' she said, having settled into the seat and rearranged her hair. On the radio, the pips signalled five o'clock and were followed by the signature tune for the news. Oblivious to the intrusive sound coming between us, she went on to explain that she'd missed the bus and had a doctor's appointment. 'At this age, all there is are complaints, son, being old is a misfortune.' 'In Galicia,' said the newsreader, 'there are approximately one million cows.' 'Of course not, madam,' I said out of politeness, 'don't say things like that.' 'Nonsense,' she said, 'they take us for a bunch of idiots. One million cows! They spend the whole day spouting nonsense.' I switched off the radio, and she turned to me with a satisfied expression. 'None of what they say is true, son, none of what they say is true.'

She asked me where I lived. I replied that I wasn't sure. 'I move about.' She smiled. 'You young ones are amazing. I lived once in Madrid. Do you know Madrid? I lived there until recently. I have a son, he went there to work and got married. One day, he turned up at home, in Soutomaior, I was peeling potatoes, and said, "Come on, mother, get your things and come with me." I replied, "What are you talking about? What am I supposed to do with the animals and the house? Who's going to look after the house?" And he said, "Don't you worry, mother, there'll be someone to look after the animals, we'll give them to the neighbours, and the house… no one's going to take the house." And so I went. I went to Madrid.'

'And did you like Madrid?'

'What?'

'Did you like Madrid?'

'A lot. I liked it a lot.'

The old woman rummaged about in her handbag and pulled out a compact mirror and some lipstick.

'I liked it a lot,' she said after doing her make-up. 'But I couldn't sleep. My son lived in an apartment, a little apartment, but it was fine. It would do. My daughter-in-law is a darling. I always wanted him to marry a local girl, but – what to do? – he married someone from over there, and I tell you that girl is amazing, very thin, but pretty all the same. She wouldn't let me lift a finger. Not even to wash the dishes. "You, mother" – she called me "mother" – "have to rest, you've already done enough work." "So have we all." "No, mother, I want you to sit down." But the problem, son, was I couldn't sleep. The walls were made of paper. The people upstairs had a child, a little baby, and of course it cried. The cot was right above my head. Can you believe those miserable parents never got up to give it some attention? Night after night, with the baby wailing out loud, until it got so tired it fell asleep, poor thing. It drove me crazy. One day, I bumped into the mother in the entrance and had a word, you bet I did. I told her they were merciless, letting a child cry like that. And do you know what the cheeky woman replied to me? "Mind your own business." That's what she said, the stupid woman. But that wasn't the worst of it.'

I glanced over. Her lips were pursed, and she was rubbing her hands.

'The worst of it was that my daughter-in-law said the same. "It has nothing to do with you, mother, everybody has to live their own life." That same night, the baby started crying. It drove me out of my wits. So I left. What do you think of that? I left the following morning.'

Passing through Meixoeiro, we saw the chaotic silhouette of Vigo in the background, a dilapidated wall in the haven of the estuary.

'Are you going to the hospital?'

'No, no. Drop me off at the entrance to Vigo, and I'll manage.'

'I can take you to the doctor, if you like. I have enough time.'

She refused again, but, when I stopped at the lights in the Praza de España, she placed a hand on my knee and leaned over as if to share a secret. 'Do you know where Nova Olimpia is?' I was surprised, but said that I did. 'Yes, I think so.' 'Then drop me off there. There's a dance for OAPs today. Did you know, when I came back from Madrid, I got myself a boyfriend?'

'I don't suppose he's a doctor?'

'No, of course not!' she said, crying with laughter.

THE SONS OF LUC & FER

Give me, black rain,
your tears.

This was our opening ballad. On the shadowy stage, Lis sang slowly, like a man possessed, wrapping the mike in the languid disorder of his mane.

Give me, white goddess,
your bitter silver.

The way he was right now, Lis failed to appreciate the hornets' nest they'd stuck us in. We sons of Luc & Fer dressed in rigorous mourning. Most of the audience – which was growing impatient with obvious smoke signals and warlike gestures – as well. Except that the black we were wearing was that of soft, existentialist wool, while theirs was of threatening imitation leather, a plastic gleam, metallic studs and an assortment of ironmongery that included legionary eagles and swastikas.

Give me, lonely heart,
your cold fire.

I desperately searched for the concert promoter. What idiot had decided to bill us as a heavy metal band? I went through our repertoire of ecological jazz, a movement of which we were neglected pioneers. The loudest thing we had was a composition that went by the title of 'Bucolic Country', where I would ring a cowbell and Lis would howl like a lunatic dog.

Give me, mother rain,
your silken lament.

After an initial moment of surprise, the audience no longer suppressed its discontent. Nature has endowed me with a special instinct to predict catastrophes, but you didn't have to be an augur to interpret the fact there was one hell of a rumpus making its way to the White Power, an old poultry farm on the dry border, which had been turned into a concert venue.

Give me, Celtic graveyard,
your peace.

'Sure you'll like it,' the promoter had said on the phone. 'We've left it practically as it was, to make it look more authentic. We hired an avant-garde architect – a genius, you'll meet him – and after six months' work he got to the conclusion that the best design was precisely that of a farm.' The aesthetic effort to keep the place looking genuine was very noticeable. The fact is they hadn't done anything except kick out the chickens and hens, judging by the number of feathers still floating inside the hall. Unaware of all this, Lis was singing in a cloud of melancholy, like an alder on the riverbank in the morning mist.

Give me, queen serpent,
your wings.

Gabino's violin was the target reached by the first beer can. Abel on sax stared at me in horror, and I saw the air leaving him in a protracted sigh, an impressive sight that can only be achieved on rare occasions. To quote the classics, the tension was so thick you could chew on it.

Give me, naked land,
your embrace.

'What shite is this, you sissies?' exclaimed one of the beasts. I felt ridiculous and defenceless with my toy drum set and chopsticks. A few more missiles landed on the stage, shells on a field of daisies.

Give me, sad god,
a curse.

Ding, dong. Lis finally unglued himself from the mike, carefully pinned his hair behind his ears and nodded gratefully as the uproar began. 'Thank you, thank you. Our next ballad is called…' Dodging the shower of cans and other, more or less solid objects, I made it over to where he was. '"Bucolic Country",' I screamed in his ear. 'Another romantic ballad,' Lis carried on, unfazed by the apocalypse. 'For the love of God, Lis, for the love of God, "Bucolic Country",' I shouted, pulling on his arm. 'They're going to kill us, Lis, don't you realize they're going to kill us?' He turned towards the audience, and one of the missiles must have whizzed straight past him because he seemed to come to. 'Jeez,' he said in amazement, 'what a strange bunch of people.' '"Bucolic Country", Lis, "Bucolic Country",' I insisted uneasily.

So it was we saved our skins in that farming venue, the White Power. With an unending song in which Lis barked like a moonstruck dog and I shook the cowbell like an irate prophet.

THE MILL

'You like the mill, don't you?'

He'd been leaning on the stone parapet of the bridge for quite some time, watching the river's waters skip over to take shelter under the arches of the riverside house.

'If you like it so much, I'll sell it to you.'

Feeling taken aback, he paid attention for the first time to this farmer watching his cattle from the side of the road, controlling them with light flicks of his stick and indecipherable cries:

'*Va ve isca Morena. Ei Linda suuu.*'

'I will, I'll sell it to you,' repeated the farmer, almost smiling because of the other man's surprise at his sudden offer. He really did feel quite taken aback. Even if he'd explained it to him, the old farmer would never have understood how much. He'd set out early that day precisely so that he could stop and survey the mill at his leisure. He'd often driven past after a weekend at his mother's house, on his way back to the city. He'd always been in a hurry, his head filled by pressing matters awaiting him on Monday. And halfway along his route, to the right of the bridge over the river Arnela, always that house erected over the waters, enveloped in moss and tied with ivy like a miraculous, soothing present.

'I can see you like it,' said the old farmer again. 'The mill's yours if you want it.'

He was about to come out with a sarcastic reply. He was a university teacher, but he wasn't naive. He could tell when somebody was pulling his leg. A farmer doesn't sell anything, not even a sick cow, just like that, without putting up a fight. But he didn't have time to react. The old peasant called for Linda and Morena and left, chuckling under his breath.

A few days later, while the students were holding a meeting to discuss the suitability of renaming the subject 'Philosophy of Science' 'Science of Philosophy', he read an ad in the classifieds that knocked him for six. For sale, the mill on Arnela Bridge, ready to be lived in, with ten ares of land. He jotted down the reference number, feeling distinctly flushed, and went down to the bar to drink a coffee. Fortunately, the student meeting had been prolonged because they were now discussing the controversial issue of faults in the heating.

In the afternoon, as soon as it reopened, he eagerly went to pay a visit to Rius Estate Agents, the company that had placed the ad. The address was on the Rúa Frei Rosendo Salvado, in the new part of town, but once there he found it difficult to locate apartment D on the right-hand mezzanine. There were no letters on the doors, and he had to knock on all of them until a woman in heavy make-up answered, taking time to puff up her hair while letting him in. The estate agent's office was so small it would have been difficult to fit a dozen brooms in it, but his hostess invited him to take a seat as if they were in the lobby of the Hotel Aragüaney.

The mill was an unmissable opportunity. That was what she said. She was sure, in her capacity as a professional, that in minutes there would be a queue stretching all the way to the Praza Roxa in response to such an unbelievable offer. He had the good fortune, nay the honour, to be first in line for the aforementioned bargain, and only a fool would let such an opportunity slip by.

'I'm going to let you in on a secret, and I ask you never to divulge this to anybody,' said Madame Rius. 'Arnela Mill belongs to a very distinguished family that finds itself in rather difficult financial circumstances. They have done away with all their other properties, but promised themselves the mill-house would be the last thing they sold. So it has been until now. Things got complicated, so at a huge sentimental cost to themselves, as you can imagine, they have come to us to ask us to oversee the transaction, provided we guarantee them absolute discretion.'

'Yes, of course, but…'

'Yes, yes, I understand. You want to know the price. I've told you it's an unmissable opportunity. You have to realize it's not really a mill, it's a small riverside palace…'

'Yes, but…'

'Judging by our experience, I can tell you offers like this are usually snapped up straight away, they're not very common. People in the country today may not know very much about anything else, but they've learned to appreciate the value of old stones, and I can tell you they always ask for ridiculous prices. You can't imagine how difficult they make it for us. The most idiotic among them talks of millions with the same familiarity as a broker on Wall Street. You can't imagine what a business it is. But Arnela Mill is different.'

He felt tempted to raise his hand so that he could speak, but Madame Rius leaned over the table, spilling perfume as she went, with the gesture of someone who is going to share a valuable secret:

'Five million.'

'Five million?'

'Five million. Aren't you surprised?'

'Well, yes, I am, the truth is it's a good price.'

'What do you mean, a good price? It's almost a present.'

'Does that include the land?'

'All ten ares of it. The lot for five million.'

'Even so, were it possible, even after what you've told me, I should like to meet the owners. I may not look it, but I'm also a country type, you know. No, no, it's not that I don't trust you. On the contrary. It's just that all of this is like a dream…'

'I can imagine,' said Madame Rius with a large grin. 'You are clearly a very sensitive person, that much is obvious. Well, we can always give it a go. I think if you're serious about the deal…'

'Of course I'm serious.'

'They'll need a sign, a small detail, to show them that an agreement has been reached. You see, we can't embarrass our clients should you decide to backtrack. That would be very unpleasant.'

'I quite understand.'

When he came back with an envelope containing two hundred thousand pesetas, in the absence of anywhere else, four or five people were standing in the corridor. In the estate agent's office, Madame Rius was negotiating with a client he immediately recognized as a professor of analytics specializing in W. One of those ancient, undeclared, impossible faculty infatuations, since he couldn't bear, let alone understand, said W. He greeted her politely and took the receipt Madame Rius held out to him with a grin.

The following day, he tried unsuccessfully on four occasions to get someone to open the door to apartment D on the right-hand mezzanine. All his attempts to find out information in the building about Rius Estate Agents were in vain. He only succeeded in getting the people in apartment A, which turned out to be the office of the United Church of Sameness, to force him to accept a leaflet on harmony and chaos. He continued seeking information in other establishments and among other estate agents, but no one had ever heard of Madame Rius. In the classified-ads section of the local newspaper, he was informed that this estate agent had only placed an advertisement for one day, precisely that day he had responded to it. When he went to the police station, the inspector who registered his complaint seemed totally unsurprised by his account.

He gazed over at a colleague sitting lazily with his feet on the desk and remarked quite openly, 'Barallobre, another clown who got done by Mata Hari.'

'Mata Hari?' he asked out of curiosity.

'That's right. We've been after her for years. At the start of the seventies, she was selling shares in telecommunications, then fishing licences in the Gran Sol, after that positions as janitor in the local government, and now it seems she's duping yuppies in real estate. We just can't catch her. She moves like a fish amongst the people.'

He wasn't at all amused to have a guardian of order quote Mao Zedong so freely and abandon his cause so easily.

'Take it with philosophy,' said the inspector.

That was all he needed. He was red with rage.

'With philosophy, my foot,' he said before leaving and slamming the door.

He went for a walk in the Alameda and thought about what had happened. In short, the purchase of a dream had cost him the equivalent of one month's salary and an article in the magazine *Paradigm* edited by the Foundation of Interbank Heterodox Culture. He wasn't a yuppie! He had a hi-fi, a video, and went travelling in summer. Those were his vices. He'd even resigned from the College of New Philosophers as soon as he turned thirty-five – unlike the president, who must be forty-six and still featured in conferences about new promises.

The following weekend, he avoided the subject in his parents' home. Some outdoor work helped him forget

Bertrand Russell's ironic smile on a poster on the wall of his university department. On his return, as he crossed Arnela Bridge, he closed his eyes and accelerated. But, after a few miles, a strange sense of remorse made him turn around. He stopped on the bridge and headed towards the mill. In the evening light, fringed by alders, it looked like an old god's music box. Sitting on the steps down to the river was a woman he quickly recognized as his colleague in analytics. He broke a leaf off an alder, folded it in his mouth and mimicked a bird call.

'Hello.'

'Hello.'

'How's W.?'

'You know, I've kind of lost interest in W.,' she said.

THE PROVINCIAL ARTIST

He had a studio next to the sea, a whole warehouse that had belonged to Coruña's slaughterhouse, all to himself. There were nights he slept there, on top of the canvases, surrounded by half-eaten cans of food, listening to the Orzán sea and ghostly roars. He lived well. In the provinces, he could sit and gaze for hours, even days, and people understood him. He was an artist, after all.

One of his paintings of happy-looking cows was chosen for an exhibition of young art, RE(CENTLY) BORN, organized by the Youth Institute, a rehash of the old Falangist Front, and was surprisingly well received in Madrid. One of the most influential critics in Spain's capital wrote a passionate eulogy of Mariano Espiña's work with the expressive title of 'BLIMEY'. 'There is in Spain,' declared the critic Bernabé Candela, 'nature and metaphysics, passion and biology, reflection and outbursts, and it is well known there is no beauty without rebellion, even if that convulsion is contained by the prudent nets of reason. Espiña may be a wonderful symbiosis, that of the monster awaiting the end of the century.' He read this article in the old slaughterhouse while peeling open a tin of mussels. His first reaction of complacent vanity was followed by a sense of disquiet and unease. Up until then, hardly anybody had paid him any attention. He was completely unknown in the world of culture. He never went to inaugurations or parties where the mayor and councillor discussed the future of culture, swapping roles, since a little earlier, in the Chamber of Commerce, they had elaborated on the future of agriculture. On the few occasions he'd attended one of these events, all he'd done was embarrass himself before his peers, especially women, since the slightest contact with the chemistry of cocktails had the effect of arousing his basest instincts.

Now a painting of his had triumphed in the capital. The rickety warehouse was besieged by local journalists, and the entire artistic world, excluding an embittered few, turned out to celebrate the birth of a new star. Even Bernabé Candela travelled by train to the provinces to see for himself the territory in which Espiña produced his portentous creatures, later publishing an extensive interview called 'TWELVE HOURS ON THE ATLANTIC EXPRESS TO REACH A SLAUGHTERHOUSE', which didn't do anything to improve the railway service, but did increase expectation about the Galician barbarian in the capital. Espiña used his long hours of self-absorption to consider a proposal the prestigious critic had made: 'Believe me, Espiña, you won't triumph unless you come to Madrid.'

He found all of this business extremely tiring. Until then, he'd felt content because during his long periods of self-absorption he thought about absolutely nothing. Now he was beset by doubt. A call from a well-known gallery owner in Madrid, whom Candela had informed about his work, finally convinced him.

A potential winner should pay attention to the details, thought Espiña. So he decided to travel without any luggage and introduce himself as a genuine artist whose only patrimony is his ingenuity. The passengers on the Atlantic Express, heading to the Estación del Norte in Madrid, didn't quite understand these circumstances and did everything they could to press against the windows, leaving a generous corridor in the carriage whenever that scruffy stranger with his traditional beret, Viking's red beard, oil-encrusted apron and sprig of gorse, passed by.

No one was waiting for the artist at the station – neither the critic who had taken him under his wing, nor the gallery owner, nor any old bureaucrat from the Youth Institute, despite the fact they'd all confirmed their presence at such a historic event. So he turned his footsteps in the direction of the Plaza de España and, on the way, had the opportunity to enter into fleeting contact with the most genuine expressions of urban culture: an unemployed man playing the accordion, an unemployed man selling postcards, an unemployed man selling poems and an unemployed man selling kidneys. On the Gran Vía, still impressed by the hospitable omens, he came across a soothing sign,

'Pension alicia' – a name that was incomplete since a fateful initial 'G' had fallen off the toponym.

Pension Galicia was run by an old woman from León who offset her love of cats against an undisguised hatred of Galicians, who, however, made up ninety percent of her clientele. Mrs Díaz de Bembibre examined the new arrival from top to bottom, east to west, and grunted in disdain when he timidly confessed his place of origin. After such a triumphal landing, Espiña endeavoured to keep a cool head. He needed an extra-long session of self-absorption.

The room he was given was a closet, the only breathing hole being the door. 'There was a window,' the landlady drily explained, 'but I had it walled up. The previous tenant, a Social Security employee, attempted to commit suicide by throwing herself into the light well. She spent ten hours, the wretch, moaning from the bottom of the well until the fire crew finally rescued her. She hadn't even broken a leg,' remarked the landlady indignantly. 'Anyway, I thought it best to do away with the window.' As she explained herself, Espiña calculated the size of the canvases he could paint in such a tiny space. Three by two? Obviously not. Where would the bed go? Possibly two by one. This was only going to be a temporary studio. He wasn't in a position right now to rent anything else.

'Are you an artist or something?'

'Yes, madam.'

'Well, don't make a mess of my room.'

Having come to an agreement, he went out into the street. He felt like an orphan in the big city. It wasn't the first time he'd been to Madrid. His best memory was of the zoo and a chimpanzee that had stirred feelings of solidarity in him.

His only bond now was the critic Candela, so he decided to meet him as soon as possible and thought the best solution would be to call him at the newspaper.

'Bernabé Candela?'

'Yes.'

'This is Espiña.'

'Espiña? Espiña, Espiña... Ah, yes, the man from Galicia! What are you doing here?'

'You know, I came to triumph.'

The silence that ensued had a sinister ring to it.

'Right, to triumph, as it should be. Listen, boy, you want some advice? Work, work, work. That's the only way to succeed. Inspiration should catch you working. Oh, and something else. Stop painting cows.'

Having said this, he mumbled something about meeting up at some time and replaced the receiver.

Mariano Espiña followed his advice to the letter. He painted day and night in that stifling cupboard. He only ever came out to eat a McChicken in the hamburger restaurant located on the ground floor of the building. He lived like a mole, never emerging from his hole and forcing his way through the mysterious world of forms. He no longer painted happy cows under a leaden sky, but fantastical fauna in a starry universe.

The accumulation of paintings presented a problem. Espiña thought about it until coming up with a brilliant solution. He talked to another guest, from Monforte de

Lemos, who agreed, on the basis of a monthly payment, to store part of the other's work in his room. Little by little, the creatures multiplied, and Espiña had to reach an agreement with other tenants without Mrs Bembibre seeming to realize people were speculating in her property. After three months of intensive creation, the artist thought the time had come to summon Bernabé Candela. The critic agreed against his will since he said he had lots of engagements at seminars, conferences, round tables – tribunes on which he was due to discuss such varied themes as TRADITION AND MODERNITY, PRIMITIVE FUTURISM, OLD ROOTS AND NEW FRONTIERS and, perhaps riskiest of all, POST, TRANS AND META AVANT-GARDE ON THE EVE OF A NEW MILLENNIUM. His verdict of the provincial artist's work could not have been more discouraging:

'For fuck's sake, Espiña, this is all very passé. All this neo-baroque was good for your compatriot Laxeiro, but things today have moved in another direction. Transavantgarde, Espiña, transavantgarde. Take this catalogue and read the foreword. Don't forget, Bonito Oliva. No, not Benito. Bonito. And make a bonfire out of all of this stuff. New art is born from purification as well. And from hard work. Let the Muses catch you working.'

Espiña returned to his shabby temple with renewed vigour, having thrown all his previous production in the bin. The world that arose now contained explosive colour, intense brushstrokes bursting with fire. He was relatively pleased with this new direction, among other things because his eyesight was getting worse, due perhaps to the low light inside the pension and an unvaried diet of McChickens. After allowing a prudent period of time to go by, without slacking off for a moment, he thought it was time for Bernabé Candela to be wowed by the intensity of his new output. But the critic again clicked his tongue:

'For God's sake, Espiña, this is about as rancid as it gets. You haven't understood a thing, and I'm not surprised, stuck in here all the time. Have you been to a single exhibition since you arrived? You have to immerse yourself in the environment, feel the vibrations. Socialize, get drunk, fornicate. An artist is not a monk. All the bustle of daily life should surface in your painting. Have you any idea what new figuration is?'

No, Espiña had no idea what it was, but he determined to find out. From that day on, Mrs Bembibre was scandalized to witness the young artist's nocturnal habits. On several occasions, he vomited on her favourite rug. He kicked the cat and, worst of all, turned up on several nights in the company of exotic women with dyed Mohicans. But he also had to paint, and he did this in such a way that he had no time to sleep and presented a lamentable appearance, with sunken eyes, an outlaw's beard and the movements of a disoriented tramp. His canvases now showed hordes of people entering and leaving the metro, lavatory doors and flashing police sirens. Bernabé was summoned again. When asking his opinion, Espiña no longer looked at him as naively and submissively as before. There was a threatening gleam emanating from the black bags under his eyes.

'Not bad, Espiña, not bad,' remarked Candela in a conciliatory fashion. 'But forgive me for saying that art nowadays, at the end of the millennium, procures the serenity of snowy peaks.'

Espiña didn't reply. He accompanied the critic to the door of his hotel and, on taking his leave, said only, 'You shall have your snowy peaks.'

That night, he painted a pure white canvas. White on top of white. He then made a cut in the palm of his hand and painted a cow with his blood. A red, happy cow in the snow.

MY FRIEND TOM

The father asked, 'Who is Tom?'

The girl, who when asked how old she was showed two tiny fingers, said, 'Why, daddy, can't you see him?'

The chubby little girl was so sure of herself she even pointed to a place between the stones on the quay, which was covered by the dull light of fish scales.

'Oh, yes, of course,' said the father. And he nodded.

The boy, who when asked how old he was now proudly stuck up four fingers, gave his father an understanding look and shrugged his shoulders like a little man.

Down in the docks was a tower of planks used by builders of traditional boats called *dornas* who still refuse to move, since there are plans to open a new mall there. 'Look,' said the father, 'a castle.'

'I want to go up it,' said the boy.

The wooden castle was the height of a man with his arms raised.

He lifted the girl up as well. 'Careful,' said the father, 'be careful.'

'I want a sword, daddy,' said the boy.

'A sword, daddy,' she asked as well.

The father glanced around him. He asked them again not to move and ran between the slipways of the old shipyard. He found two firework sticks. They land over there, having left a wake of exploding lights in the two skies of the city.

'Here are your swords,' he said with a smile.

'What about Tom?' asked the girl. 'Tom doesn't have a sword.'

Father and son looked at each other.

'Ah, yes, of course,' he said, 'a sword for Tom.'

He ran to fetch another stick and placed it on top of the platform. The girl gave a satisfied smile, lifted her sword and shouted, 'Attack!' The boy did the same, but suddenly turned to face his father.

'That one is the biggest,' he said.

'That what?' his father asked.

'Tom's sword. It's bigger than mine.'

The father took the third stick and swapped it with the boy's. But then the girl burst into tears.

'What's the matter now?' asked the father.

'Mine is the smallest,' said the girl.

So the father gave her the boy's one and placed hers on top of the wood.

'I'm a dragon,' he said.

The children turned to face him with their artificial weapons.

'Now you have to chase the dragon,' the father said. He climbed down from the wooden tower and ran off to hide behind the skeleton of a half-finished *dorna*. The children approached, pretending to be skilled fencers. The father raised his head and let out a hoarse cry.

'I'm the fire-breathing dragon,' he said.

'No,' said the boy, 'you're an ogre.'

'All right then, I'm an ogre.'

'No, I don't want you to be an ogre,' said the girl.

'I can always be an ogreish dragon,' said the father in a conciliatory tone.

The children lowered their swords and seemed to be wondering whether that was an acceptable kind of monster.

The girl suddenly turned towards the tower.

'Tom, daddy!' she sobbed, 'Tom's going to fall!'

The father ran off in the direction of the castle and pretended to rescue Tom.

'The sword, Tom's sword!' shouted the girl.

'What if we give Tom a ride on the boat,' said the father on his return.

'All right,' said the boy, squeezing between the ribs of the future *dorna*. 'Let's go fishing!'

'We'll catch a big fish,' said the father.

'Sharks,' said the boy.

'Whales,' said the girl.

'My rod is the biggest,' said the boy. 'Isn't it?'

'Of course it is,' said the father, 'but hers is big as well.'

'And Tom's,' said the girl. 'Tom's is big, isn't it?'

'They're all big,' said the father.

'My rod, my rod!' shouted the boy. It had fallen on the ground, and he was trying to get it back by stretching out his arms.

'Careful, you might fall into the sea!' said the father in alarm. He then asked for the girl's and with the third rod made a pair of scissors with which to pick up the one that had fallen. 'That's it,' said the father, 'now hold on to it, fishermen mustn't let go of their rods.'

'OK,' said the boy, clenching his teeth and fingers as he gazed out over the stone sea.

'A whale!' shouted the girl. 'Daddy, a whale. Look, Tom, I caught a whale.'

The father stretched out his arms and made a great effort to haul the specimen in.

'Daddy, daddy!' shouted the boy. 'The sharks are here!'

The father helped the boy to hold on to the rod, and together they pulled slowly as if a great force were resisting them from the ground.

'There it is at last!' said the father. 'Wow, that's a big one.'

'My shark's bigger than the whale, isn't it?' asked the boy.

'Not bigger, but stronger. And more dangerous.'

'Daddy, daddy!' the girl shouted again. 'Tom's caught the big fish! Help, daddy, help!!'

'Now that really is a big one,' said the father.

'But it's not as strong as my shark, is it?' asked the boy.

'No,' agreed the father, 'it's not as strong as your shark or as big as the whale.'

The pilot boat approached the docks. The neon lights of banks gleamed from the roofs of the city.

'Come on, it's late,' said the father. 'We'll have to stop fishing.' He took the girl in his arms and let the boy go first, slicing the wind with his stick that had turned back into a sword. They walked for ten minutes and, as they approached the house, the girl burst into tears.

'What is it now?' asked the father.

'Daddy,' sobbed the girl uncontrollably, 'we left Tom inside the boat. We left Tom all alone at sea.'

'Why's the girl crying?' asked the mother.

'Oh, nothing, she's just tired,' the father replied.

COTTON FIELDS

The third company, in sports clothes, lined up on the parade ground. It was pouring down, and the raindrops slid across the troops' stiffly raised faces. The third company was a perfect machine. Even after they were discharged, the soldiers could not permit themselves the vengeful act of hanging their locks on the steel wire that supported the telegraph pole on the side of the bridge over the river Urumea. This pleasure was forbidden to them for the simple reason that the third company's private booths didn't have locks.

Mid-afternoon, life in the barracks entrenched itself behind the windows. But nothing in the world, not even accursed water, would alter the third company's training programme. Impassive under the flood, Captain Aguirre barked orders that echoed imperiously down the colonnades. According to Captain Aguirre, there were two kinds of men in the barracks: the soldiers of the third company and the others, a confused mix of skivers, idlers and queens.

Having been assigned to the telephone exchange, I

was one of the others. Needless to say, on that filthy afternoon, from behind the window of the exchange, I thanked my lucky stars that I was only half a man. Until the bell rang, a noisy buzzer that warned of an incoming call.

'Infantry barracks, how can I help you?'

'Is José there?' asked the distant voice of a woman.

'José? What José?'

'José, is that you? Can you put José on the line?'

'What José, madam? There are lots of Josés here.'

'I wanted José to be given leave. It's for the cotton, you know. For harvesting the cotton.'

'I can't transfer your call, madam. You'll have to call later, after half past six.'

'My husband's sick. Please let José come. It's for the cotton.'

'Which José do you want to talk to, madam? I'll take a message and, if you call back later, you'll be able to talk to him. But you have to give me his surname. We have lots of Josés.'

'It's for the cotton, you know. We need him.'

'I'm afraid I can't help you with that, madam. I'm the telephone operator.'

'A fortnight. It's for the cotton.'

'Just a moment, madam, just a moment.'

The buzzer had sounded again, and the colonel's light was flashing on the electric switchboard.

'At your orders, colonel!'

'Put me through to headquarters in Burgos.'

'Yes, colonel. At once, colonel.'

I pressed outside line number 5, secretly hoping they'd have hung up. But they hadn't.

'Listen, listen. Don't cut me off. I walked miles to make this call. Please just let José come. It's for the cotton.'

'Madam, I already told you I'm the phone operator. I can't grant him leave. If you call back after half past six…'

'You sound like a nice person. Have a heart. Let him come. He'll be back in a fortnight.'

'Please, madam, listen to what I'm saying. I…'

The buzzer kept sounding. The colonel's light flashed wildly on the switchboard.

'At your orders, colonel.'

'What happened to that call to headquarters?'

'The line is engaged, colonel. I'll keep on trying, colonel.'

The light on line 5 was still lit, fluttering its wings like an uneasy butterfly. I pressed down hard on it, hoping to silence it for ever.

'Madam? Are you still there, madam?'

'Don't cut me off, please. I walked for miles.'

'For goodness' sake, madam, this is the telephone exchange. I am the phone operator. Do you understand? I'm just the phone operator.'

'It doesn't matter to you. One more or less won't make a difference. But we need José to harvest the cotton.'

'Tell me his name, madam. His whole name. Do you understand? His full name. Tell me your son's surname.'

'Will you let him out?'

'Listen, you have to tell me what José is called. I can't

do anything if you don't tell me what he's called…'

'José.'

'Yes, José. What else? What else, madam?'

'García.'

'José García García?'

'That's right, José García. Will you let him come? He needs to be here on Wednesday. When will you let him out?'

I could see her face, white hair, about fifty, clinging to the phone, staring at the metal plate in the booth. The colonel's light brought me back to reality.

'It's engaged, colonel. It's still…'

'What the hell is going on with that call, soldier?'

'It's still engaged, colonel. I'll try again, colonel.'

He grunted and hung up. I decided to forget about line 5 and dialled headquarters in Burgos. Heavens above, it was engaged. Out on the parade ground, the men of the third company were splashing about in the puddles, their legs all covered in mud. My finger trembled when I pressed line 5. She was still there. I could hear her breathing.

'Madam,' I whispered.

'Can José come?' she asked anxiously.

'Madam, I have to know what company José's in. Tell me what company he's in.'

'Infantry, don't you know my José? He's in infantry.'

'We're all in infantry, madam. These are the infantry barracks.'

I was about to shout. My head was dizzy. That was when the door of the exchange burst open. I jumped to my feet and saluted nervously.

'What's going on with that call to Burgos, soldier?'

'It's engaged, colonel. I swear it's engaged. It's not usual, colonel, but it's been engaged all this time. I'll try again.'

He prepared to wait next to the telephone, glancing distrustfully at the switchboard. I dialled from memory. The call connected.

'At last, sir. Headquarters. Shall I put it through to your office?'

He took the receiver without a word. He decided to talk from there. He discussed what had happened at the races, and his bad-tempered face grew happy, while I stood to attention, watching the light on line 5 slowly fade like a bird.

SUNDAY

The bumper cars moved with the rhythm of a poor waltz, with thick lips and indiscreet watercolours, as if they'd come straight out of a Disney cartoon with innocent furore. In chains of wind, ash-grey and snow-white, the teenage girls flashed skirts and smiles.

'How's it going, champ?' said Fredo.

Mini returned his greeting with his left hand. A blow that stroked his chin.

'Hey,' said Fredo, 'nice day.'

'I thought it would rain,' said Mini. 'I spent the whole morning in bed. When the old woman arrived, I was still in bed. She gave me a right talking-to.'

'I went fishing,' said Fredo. 'With my brother.'

'I didn't eat or anything, not after the fuss that woman kicked up.'

'You have such fun when you're fishing. There's a dump that empties into the sea, and it's full of mullets. Mullets everywhere. Sticking out their heads.'

'You can't imagine what she's like when she gets going. She called me a "son of a bitch". I said if I was a son of a bitch, then that made her a bitch. She could have killed me.'

'There were mullets everywhere. I felt like stoning them.'

'I left home in such a rush I didn't even have time to grab my jacket.'

'Another time, we're going fishing for pouting. You have to go by boat. My brother knows a place that's teeming with them because there's a ship graveyard down at the bottom.'

'She blames me for messing up the television, she blames me for everything. Like I'm the devil or something. That woman's unbearable.'

'Fish breed a lot better on scrap metal. You can't cast a net down there. It gets caught on the metal and fucked.'

'How many did you catch?'

'How many what?'

'Mullets, you idiot. Didn't you say you went fishing for mullets?'

'Oh, none.'

'None? Not a single one?'

'No, none. My brother did, he kicked them. I kept getting the line caught. It's full of cans and shit like that. I got fed up and decided to leave it. I'm just glad we took a bottle with us. You wouldn't believe the way the mullets pop up their heads, with bulging eyes and sharp teeth. If you throw a fag end in the water, they rush towards it.'

'Did they bite you?'

'You bet they fucking did. But then they let go. My brother said he gave them a yank and broke their jaws. But I'd never been before.'

'How's it going?' said Tito, who had just arrived.

'OK,' said Fredo.

'Fucked,' said Mini, who danced around him like a boxer.

'One, two, three… kicks in the balls,' said Tito, playing along.

Mini jumped back in time to grab his leg.

'Hey, watch it, you'll have me over!' shouted Tito, trying to keep his balance.

Mini finally let go, and they both burst out laughing.

'Fuck me, did you see those reflexes?' said Mini after letting go.

'Where are the others?' Tito asked Fredo.

'Don't know. It's still a bit early.'

'We could always have a drink,' suggested Tito.

'I think it might be better to wait here,' said Fredo, chewing gum and shifting around uneasily.

'Is your brother coming?'

'Don't think so,' said Fredo, gazing into the distance.

'He's after a girl,' said Mini with a wink.

'You what?' exclaimed Tito disbelievingly. The three of them fell silent.

'About time!' shouted Tito with sudden delight.

'Fuck, Quique, you're turning into a skeleton,' said Mini, sinking his fingers into the new arrival's generous belly.

'Go take it up the bum,' said Quique, pushing him away. 'You know they're letting him off his military service, but I can't say whether it's because they think he's a midget or a queen.'

'When are you leaving?' asked Fredo seriously.

'In a month, I think,' said Mini.

'Mini the parachutist! What a lark!' said Quique.

'I'm going to get a tattoo right here before I go,' said Mini, pointing to his groin.

'Oh, yeah? What are you going to have done?' asked Quique.

'Your sister's fanny.'

Mini dodged the friendly swipe and cracked up laughing.

'Six months, right?' asked Fredo.

'I think so,' said Mini, 'but I plan to stay. That's why I'm volunteering.'

'What's the old woman say?'

'She's off her head,' said Mini, spitting on the ground. 'Can't understand a word she's saying. She's lost her mind. She thinks I messed up the television because of the video and all that.'

'But does she know you're joining the paras?'

'Course she does. I don't know. I think so, I may have said something about it.'

'Is your brother coming?' Quique asked Fredo.

'Don't think so,' said Fredo.

'He got himself hooked up,' said Tito.

'Is that right, Fredo?'

'Don't know. Maybe.'

'What's up, you bunch of losers?' said Barcia, whom they called Indie, the last to arrive.

'Well, here we all are,' said Mini.

'What about your brother?' Indie asked Fredo.

'Don't think he's coming,' said Fredo, shrugging his shoulders.

'He has the hots for some girl,' said one of the others.

'No kidding!' exclaimed Indie.

'So what are we doing?' asked Fredo, who seemed to want to move.

'Just a moment! Look over there!' said Mini, pointing to a couple snogging next to a shooting gallery.

'Look, Fredo, it's your brother.'

'The girl's a looker.'

'She's fucking gorgeous.'

'Hey, Miguel!'

'Keep it down, for fuck's sake,' said Mini.

'So then,' said Fredo, looking annoyed. 'Where are we going?'

'That's right,' said one of the others, 'where the fuck are we going?'

MADONNA (CHRISTMAS STORY)

I am fifteen, almost sixteen, in year 11. I live in a village, my parents have a dairy farm. Almost everybody around here has cows. There are even triangular road signs to warn about cows. The teachers come from the city every morning in their cars. They used to be in such a hurry they didn't even see the signs. Now, suddenly, everybody's got cows on the mind. They've turned into strange creatures. They appear on television surrounded by guards, like criminals chewing drugs, the cameras focus on them so closely they deform their faces, like somebody uncovering a dangerous network of quadruped psychopaths hiding in the dark sties of the West.

We were given an essay to do on mad cow disease, and I felt terrible. Another strange beast. I'd rather have a detention or an exercise about square roots. I couldn't start writing. I've heard so much about it these days a clapper of bone seems to ring in the bell of my memory:

spong i form
en ce pha lo pa thy

I could even write down its scientific name. But grandpa said never to call Satan by his name. He was an emigrant in Argentina and called him Lazybones or Shorty. I don't know how to write to drive away such a terrible disease. I'd like to write backwards, as they say people do in some languages.

If I wrote backwards, I could tell you about Dosinda, the old blind woman who used to milk her only cow, Mulberry. Nobody else was allowed to touch Mulberry's udders. She would do it every night, just before dawn. Whenever somebody else tried to milk the cow, her teats would dry up. So we could say the milk belonged equally to the cow's teats and Dosinda's hands. The first light of day was the bucket of milk the blind woman carried out of the shed.

Last year, the Maths teacher told us all about negative numbers. I couldn't get my head around them. Negative numbers exist, but they don't exist. The teacher told me to think about a debt. That's a negative number. Can you put a negative sign, a minus sign, in front of people? I suppose so, when they're dead, like Dosinda and Mulberry. For me, they haven't disappeared, so I suppose they're 'minus two'. But it's not just dead people who are negative numbers. On my parents' farm, there are fourteen cows, and they're always being told that this isn't a profitable number, the minimum to survive is twenty or more. So my parents have 'minus six cows'. Up until now, we all had a negative number of cows. There were too many people and not enough heads of cattle. That's what we kept being told in offices, banks and newspapers. Farms had to be like factories, and cows were motionless, feeding machines for the multiplication of kilos and milk. Otherwise, they said, we'd all end up as negative numbers.

The local towns and villages are being populated by negative numbers. It's supposedly like that all over Galicia. I love my parents, but there are times, when I'm dozing on the school bus, I dream the bus doesn't stop, we grow older along the way, and it takes us to Switzerland, London, Barcelona or the Canaries. I have a cousin in Barcelona who's a hairdresser. I'd like to be more like her. I'm so timid I envy her her brashness. In the summer, at a dance, a young man said to her, 'You have very pretty eyes.' And she replied, 'What you want is a fuck, right?' The guy couldn't believe his ears!

It was she who baptized our blonde cow Madonna. The name stuck. Even though she has an ear tag with the identification number EU-LU-2091C. This makes her look more ugly. The vet says it's like our identity cards. But we don't carry our personal numbers stapled to our heads.

My favourite teacher is the Art teacher. One day, he talked to us about warm and cold colours. The warmest colour I know is that of Madonna. I write backwards and remember her first delivery. It was on Christmas Eve last year. We were all very worried about the coincidence. Besides, it was cold, and the wind played the tuneless harmonica of the roof like a whistle. My father said, before the birth, it was going to be a good calf. He'd stuck his arm inside the cow and stroked the calf's eyes. They were already blinking. That's a good sign – if the one that's going to be born can already open its eyes in the loving darkness of its mother's stomach.

On farms, when a calf is born, the mother is not allowed to see it. Or lick it. If you let that happen, the cow won't give any milk, it will keep it all for the calf. Even if it dies, a cow can keep on giving milk for several hours so the calf will survive. The Art teacher says there are subjective colours as well. For example, mourning can be white or black, depending on the country. I reckon the dead cow's milk is emerald green, and that way the calf suckles the last grass its mother grazed on.

On Christmas Eve, my father took the calf out of Madonna's sight – I don't know whether she was dead or not, but she certainly looked it – hung it up by its paws and slapped it like an enormous baby. My mother, that day, was in a strange mood. She said to him, 'Let the calf go and suck its mother's milk!' When my mother's like that, she can see in the dark like blind Dosinda.

Read more Galician fiction in English from Small Stations Press:

Suso de Toro, POLAROID

One of the most exciting works of literature to have come out of Galicia in the last thirty years, and the first adult-fiction title by Suso de Toro to be made available in the English-language market. There is something startling about this book. With Raymond Carver-like simplicity, the author extracts the commonplace events and ordinary frustrations of life, shedding light on them, exalting them and undermining them at the same time, so that the reader is left in a hiatus, expectant and fulfilled. What goes on here is impossible, outrageous, and yet it happens. A blind man beats and is poisoned by his wife, an aged housemaid tries to breastfeed the baby when the parents are out, a second-hand typewriter insists on typing out its own message, a rapist awaits the family's vengeance while wishing he knew the victim's name, a cash machine flirts with a customer of the bank by making spurious deposits into her account, a jumper turns murderous, a porn model seeks an intimate relationship that isn't confined to the glossy pages of a magazine, a mother loses track of her child, Cain and Abel appear in modern dress, the hero Theseus is driven to question whether he really is a hero or not, a man finds his wife having an affair in the wardrobe... There is something absolutely surprising about these stories that signalled a new direction in post-Franco Galician literature, in a book the author himself described as 'an outburst of fury inspired by punk.'

ISBN 978-954-384-036-6

Miguel-Anxo Murado, SOUNDCHECK:

TALES FROM THE BALKAN CONFLICT
The death of a foreign cameraman outside Karlovac, the threat of Serbian snipers in Zagreb, a massacre of village peasants by guerrilla fighters, a young Croat who joins forces with a Serbian scrap merchant and is caught up in a confrontation with Gypsies competing for scrap metal left over by the war... The stories in Miguel-Anxo Murado's *Soundcheck: Tales from the Balkan Conflict* focus on the hostilities between Croats and Serbs during the 1991 war in Croatia. Told with chilling brevity and disarming intensity, the stories bring to life a conflict the author himself covered as a foreign correspondent and are based on real-life events or conversations that took place during the war. Miguel-Anxo Murado, a regular contributor to *The New York Times* and *The Guardian* newspapers, is known for his fiction based on his experiences as a journalist in war-torn regions of the world, from the ex-Yugoslavia to the Middle East. Inspired by fleeting conversations or poignant scenes, he draws universal lessons about the nature and ultimate destiny of humankind.

ISBN 978-954-384-037-3

Xurxo Borrazás, VICIOUS

Shakespearean drama set in a Galician context. There is something strikingly postmodern – or Elizabethan – about this novel, in which a man from Laracha, south-west of Coruña, on Galicia's famed Coast of Death, is on the run for committing a multiple murder that shocks the local community and has the priest calling for the razing of the local slums. Chucho Monteiro, who has always been overlooked by his father in favor of his younger brother, Daniel, more pliable, less violent, heads to the port of Coruña in order to effect his escape on the first ship weighing anchor, a ship that will take him not to Stratford, but to Southampton and on. In a fascinating, multi-layered narrative, the author keeps the reader guessing about the murderer's final destination until the very end. Narrative chronology is mixed up, and the veil between author and reader is torn in two, so that we're not sure if we are witnesses or partakers of this narrative. *Vicious* (called *Criminal* in Galician) is Xurxo Borrazás' second and best-known novel, and won him the Spanish Critics' Prize as well as the San Clemente Prize awarded by high-school readers.

ISBN 978-954-384-038-0

Agustín Fernández Paz, BLACK AIR

Víctor Moldes is an outstanding psychiatry student, looking to test his knowledge on patients. He is given a job at the prestigious Beira Verde Clinic in Galicia, near the Portuguese border, and handed a patient, Laura Novo, who is capable only of writing her name on blank sheets of paper. Slowly he draws her out of herself and she agrees to tell him her story, how she left Madrid in order to work on her thesis and escape a difficult relationship that was going nowhere. Her return to the land where she grew up, to stay in a guest house run by a schoolteacher she had fallen passionately in love with when she was a teenager, has fatal consequences. Her presence in the remote area of Terra Chá awakens the Great Beast, who up until that moment had been slumbering in the depths of the earth. Once awake, the Great Beast has one year to achieve its objective. Dr Moldes finds himself drawn into a conflict he is barely able to understand, let alone control, and, having finally pieced together the fragments of the narrative, he is in a race against time to save his patient.

ISBN 978-954-384-028-1

Fina Casalderrey, DOVE AND CUT THROAT

André Santomé Lobeira is a teenager whose parents divorced when he was five. He puts on a front at school to defend himself against the bullies Raúl Pernas and Héctor Solla, who do everything they can to make his life miserable. He starts deliberately getting low marks in the hope they will ignore him. This encourages his grandfather to intervene, and André goes to live with his grandparents, who run a restaurant, *The Birdhouse*, in the garden of which his grandfather has an orphanage for birds. André finds a baby cut-throat finch, a finch with a red line across its neck, and keeps it as a pet. He is torn between two girls – Halima, a Moroccan girl in his class whose mother died as they were crossing into Spain, who helps him stand up to the bullies; and Dove, a girl he meets on the Internet, who helps him with his homework and when his grandfather falls ill. Dove arranges for them to meet in person, but André is afraid this will ruin their friendship and feels a strange sense of betrayal to the other girl in his life, Halima. He almost wishes Dove had never arranged their meeting…

ISBN 978-954-384-029-8

Marcos Calveiro, THE PAINTER WITH THE HAT OF MALLOWS

A teenage boy is sent by his mother to spend a few days in the country as a way of getting him out of trouble. In the town of Auvers-sur-Oise, one hour north of Paris, the boy finds life with his great-aunt unbearable – that is until the arrival of the painter Vincent van Gogh, who has come to escape difficulties in the south. It is the summer of 1890 and already eight months have passed since the boy left his mother. He begins a friendship with the painter, taking him to places he hasn't seen and engaging in conversations that open his eyes to a different way of viewing the world, bringing to an end his turbulent past. He also struggles with the reasons for his mother's disappearance from the town where she grew up and experiences the first embers of romantic love when he develops an interest in the daughter of van Gogh's innkeeper, Adeline. Based on real events, this imaginative story of a teenage boy's friendship with an inspired painter and participation in the events of a provincial town, where he meets the local doctor, a war hero, and railway pointsman, as well as the man who could turn out to be his real father, rushes to its inevitable conclusion like the trains that slice through the countryside on their way to Paris.

ISBN 978-954-384-030-4

Elena Gallego Abad, DRAGAL I:

THE DRAGON'S INHERITANCE

After the death of his father in a caving accident, Hadrián is forced to move to Galicia with his mother and start at a new school. His mother gives him a medallion that belonged to his father, showing a dragon in a threatening posture on one side and the same dragon incubating an egg on the other. When the dragon's tails move, the boy realizes this is no ordinary medallion. Meanwhile, he has noticed the stone effigy of a dragon on the cornice of St Peter's Church, which winks at him and infiltrates his thoughts. The boy's destiny, it seems, is to sacrifice himself so that the dragon can come back to life after an interval of a thousand years, during which it has been protected in the catacombs under the church. The boy and his classmate Mónica will first have to locate the catacombs with the help of the parish priest, Father Xurxo, before they can ascertain whether the dragon's existence is for real.

ISBN 978-954-384-031-1

For an up-to-date list of our publications, please visit
www.smallstations.com

For more information on Galician literature in English, please visit
www.galicianliterature.com

www.ingramcontent.com/pod-product-compliance
Lightning Source LLC
Chambersburg PA
CBHW03052726026
47157CB00005B/1916